For The Love of Art

ANNA ELIZABETH

Copyright © [2024] by [Anna Elizabeth]

All rights reserved.

No portion of this book may be reproduced in any form without written permission from the publisher or author, except as permitted by U.S. copyright law.

Published by Jo Ann Gray

Contents

For The Love of Art   1

Poem: Love of Art & Loss   38

Fullpage image   40

For The Love of Art

Rebecca stepped off the bus at Port Authority, her heart racing with dreams as vibrant as the city's skyline. Fresh from Alabama, she was determined to make a name for herself in the art world. The bustling streets of New York felt strangely alive, buzzing with energy and possibility. With a sketchbook tucked under her arm and a portfolio of paintings in her bag, she navigated through the throngs of various people, her pulse syncing with the city's heartbeat. As Rebecca made her way out of the bus terminal, she was greeted by towering skyscrapers that loomed over her like silent giants, casting shadows that seemed to dance with the lights and neon signs. The streets were busy, loud, cars honking, people talking, the faint rhythm of a street performer's drumbeat echoing in the distance. She took a deep, calming, breath, the air thick with the smell of street food mingling with the unmistakable aroma of the subway, gasoline, and a hint of something sweet that she couldn't quite place. Passing a hot dog stand with a short, chubby man who wore a bandana over his brow and a cigar hanging from his lips, Rebecca decided to try a famous, heard-of, New

York hot dog. After her first bite into this hot dog, she was amazed. It really was delicious!

This wasn't Alabama; this place was something entirely different. Her nerves tingled with excitement, a slight fear, and the sheer thrill of adventure. For as long as she could remember, New York had always called to her, its siren song promising an escape from the quiet towns and the slower pace of life she'd known. Back home, she was always 'the artist', the girl who spent hours alone, painting the world she wished to see, but here, she was one among millions, another face in the massive crowd. She was anonymous, and she liked that. It meant she could start fresh, be who she chose to be, free of expectations or labels. She was just Rebecca, a girl chasing her dream. In the moments, she paused to take in her massive surroundings of the city, it seemed to swirl around her, its extreme energy relentless. She felt both small and invincible, like she had been handed a blank canvas, the size of Manhattan itself, and she knew one thing for sure, this was where she was meant to be, she could feel it.

Armed with a crumpled map and an address scrawled on a piece of wrinkled paper, Rebecca started walking. Her new apartment building wasn't far, but the city's streets were like a maze, each turn leading her somewhere unexpected. Crowds flowed around her like rivers, carrying her along one moment and leaving her stranded the next. She paused at a deserted corner, trying to get her bearings, glancing between her map and the street signs that seemed to be placed just out of reach, taunting her. "Need some help, sweetheart?" a man's voice called out. Rebecca looked up, startled, to see an older man in a wrinkled suit, his face seemed kind but worn. She nodded, grateful, relieved, as he pointed her in the right direction, sending her off with a chuckle and a pat on the shoulder. Little, rare, moments like these, the kindness of just a few strangers in the city of large crowds of people, the excessive noise, the unpredictability, already made her feel like she was part of something bigger, better.

After a few more wrong turns, Rebecca finally spotted the apartment building's sign, faded and peeling but standing proud above a narrow doorway. She took a deep breath of relief before stepping inside, feeling a new sense of accomplishment. It wasn't much, but it was her first small victory since she arrived in the city that would come to define her. The building inside was as she had expected, a little rundown, slightly crowded, but full of various character. The small lobby was a mishmash of old faded couches and mismatched chairs, a few travelers or locals lingered, lounging with backpacks at their feet, some reading, others staring into space with a tired yet content expression. She made her way to front desk, checked in, received her keys, and climbed the narrow staircase to her room, her new home.

Before entering her apartment, the neighbor across the hall stepped out, a woman with blue hair and a nose ring, glanced up from the book she was holding to her face as she shut her door behind her, she smiled, offering a brief nod, and then made her leave past Rebecca. Rebecca took this as a good sign, she wasn't looking for any friendships yet, just a place to catch her breath and lay her head, to get settled and familiar first. The room was small as stepped into the doorway of the apartment, shutting the door behind her. It was fully furnished with cheap furniture and appliances, the queen-size bed was vague and crammed against the wall, just enough space for a couple of suitcases to fit in the drawers of the faint dressers. As she unpacked her bags, pulling out her sketchbook and setting on the dusty bed, she allowed herself a small smile. This was her new life now, even if it seemed to be rough around the edges. That night, as she lay in the darkness of her apartment, listening to the distant sounds and hums of the city through the thin walls, she made a promise to herself, no matter what, she would make this work. She would not cry; she would not run off just because it seems tough.

    The next morning, Rebecca awoke with a renewed sense of purpose. After a quick shower, she grabbed her coffee and a bagel from her luggage, but realized there was not a coffee pot in the apartment. So, she decided to grab a coffee from one of the nearby coffee shops. She set out to explore Manhattan's art galleries. She'd mapped them out, just a few places she really wanted to see, smaller galleries that might be less intimidating than the big names. The first gallery she visited was in Chelsea, a small, modern space that featured emerging artists. The pieces were bold, abstract, and unapologetic, the kind of art that challenged her own ideas about painting. She wandered through the place in awe, studying each individual piece, trying to understand the emotions and techniques behind them. Her hands itched to paint, inspired by the daring colors and shapes she saw in each painting. As the day went on, her excitement gave way to something else, doubt. 'What if her art, her paintings, weren't good enough to be displayed next to these amazing pieces?' The more galleries she visited, the more she felt a gap between her work and what she would see on display. These artists had unique styles that were raw, complex, with layers that hinted at untold stories, untold talents. Compared to them, her work felt... much to safe.

    At one gallery, she mustered up the courage to introduce herself to the estranged owner, an older woman with piercing eyes and a sharp tone. Rebecca handed her a sample from her portfolio, holding her breath as the woman flipped through it. Finally, the woman looked up and said, "It's nice work, but nice doesn't make you a true artist. In New York, honey, nice doesn't seem to make it. Find within yourself, something that hurts, something that scares you, place that on your canvas, then, maybe you'll have something worth showing."

The words stung, but they stayed with her. The woman's honesty, it hurt a little, but Rebecca knew it was true words spoken to her. That night, as she walked back to her apartment, she turned those words over in her mind. Maybe she had been afraid to dig within herself too deep, to paint the things that truly unsettled her, but if that was what it took to make it here, she was willing to try.

The following day, while wandering through the Lower East Side, Rebecca came across a young street artist painting a mural on a brick wall. His strokes were bold, almost reckless, seeming to be done with much ease, but they formed something powerful and very beautiful. She stood watching, mesmerized, until he noticed her. "Take a picture, lady, it will last longer... Do you like it?" he asked, a sly smile playing on his lips.

She nodded, not sure if he was being rude or genuine, "It's incredible. I don't know how you do it, painting with such ease like that, out here, with everyone watching you."

He shrugged, "You learn to tune out all the noise, the people, besides, this city... It will eat you alive, lady, if you don't put yourself out there. I mean, you have to be bold, and just do it."

They started talking, and Rebecca learned that his name was Leo, and he'd been living in New York for many years, carving out his place in the city's underground art scene. He told her stories bout late-night gatherings of various artists within the city, about the raw, unfiltered work that came from those who had nothing to lose. Before they parted ways, Leo invited her to one of the gatherings, "It's not a fancy gallery," he said, "but it's where real, true art happens. If you are serious about making it in this town, you'll want to see this side of the city."

That night, Rebecca found herself in a dimly lit, abandoned warehouse, the walls covered in much graffiti and the floors littered with paint cans and used brushes. Artists of all kinds filled the place, painters, poets, musicians, each one more eccentric than the last. The air seemed thick with much creativity, and for the first time, Rebecca felt like she was exactly where she was supposed to be, she felt a calmness settle within her. She watched as artists painted directly onto the faded walls, their hands moving with severe confidence that she truly admired. There was no hesitation, no fear of any judgement. A musician across the room, played a haunting melody on his guitar, while a poet recited verses that echoed through the entire dwelling, each word heavy with much meaning. Rebecca took out her sketchbook, her fingers moving almost of their own accord as she tried to capture the energy around her. She sketched the many faces of the various people in the room, the way they held themselves, the intensity in their eyes as they performed their talents of art. She realized that this was what she'd been missing, the rawness, the fearlessness.

In the days that followed, Rebecca visited more galleries within the city, putting herself out there, even when it felt terrifying, but the city was cruel, it seemed, relentless. Gallery after gallery turned her down, rejecting her art, each rejection hitting her harder than the last. One curator even went as far as to tell her, "Your work feels too... Southern. It doesn't have the edge we look for here."

Rebecca walked out of that particular gallery feeling more lost, more hurt, than ever. Homesickness gnawed at her, memories of Alabama, her hometown, creeping into her mind unbidden. She missed the slower pace, the open spaces, the warmth of the people and her family, the ones who knew her by name. New York was vast, ruthless, unfeeling, and she was just one small person trying to make her mark in this life, but as she sat on a bench in Central Park, watching the bust world go by, she reminded herself of why she'd come here in the first place. She hadn't left everything behind just to give up now. If New York demanded an edge, she'd find it deep within herself. If the city wanted something raw, she'd dig deeper, paint the parts of herself she'd kept hidden. Rebecca returned to her apartment that night with a new resolve. She took out her paints, setting up a makeshift studio in her tiny dwelling. As spread her canvases across the floor, she began to paint... Not the serene landscapes that she was known for, but something much different. Something fierce, tangled, and messy.

She painted her doubts, her inner fears, the way the city made her feel both alive and small, invisible. She painted the loneliness of the massive crowds, the beauty in the grime, the ache of wanting something so badly that it hurt deeply. When she finally stepped back, exhausted, she realized that she'd just created something brand new, something that felt honest. New York had challenged her, broken her down, but it had also forced her to confront parts of herself she had never known. She wasn't just an amateur artist from Alabama anymore. She was Rebecca, a true, genuine, artist finding her rightful place in New York, one brushstroke at a time.

Weeks later, after countless rejections, Rebecca held to her confidence and her desire, she held to her faith in her work, and finally landed a job at Verve Gallery, a modest yet charming art gallery in the heart of Chelsea. Verve Gallery wasn't like the high-end, aloof galleries that had dismissed her without a second thought. This art gallery, with its slightly worn floors and exposed brick walls, had an estranged personality all its own. Its walls were adorned with an electric mix of various works, from established names to emerging voices. Rebecca could sense that Verve Gallery wasn't just about the art, it was about the stories, the voices, the meanings, and the journeys of the artists.

The gallery owner, named Charlie, had been hesitant at first, when she'd showed him her portfolio, flipping through her rogue pieces with a look of quiet concentration. Charlie was tall, with tousled blonde hair and an aura of intensity that made her pulse quicken, "Just a few for now, Miss Rebecca," he had said, finally, after a long pause of silence, "Let's see how these do, first." His gaze lingered on her work, as if he was searching for something deeper within the strokes and colors.

It seemed to be only after nightfall that Charlie would appear, slipping into the gallery as if he were a shadow. He spoke little, but he listened intently, his dark eyes piercing in a way that made her feel seen and vulnerable all at once. There was something magnetic about him, something she couldn't quite put her finger on, and as the weeks passed, she found herself drawn to him in ways she hadn't expected. She found herself seeking his approval over her art, yet she did not understand why she needed it so badly. Still, each time Charlie would invite her to dinner, she would politely decline, masking her desire behind a polite smile, "I'm here to focus on my art, and my art only," Rebecca would say, brushing off the flicker of excitement his invitations stirred in her. But Charlie was persistent, "Art can be shared, Miss Rebecca," he'd reply softly, a hint of a challenge in his tone, and each time, it left her wondering what exactly he was offering to share.

Rebecca's days at Verve Gallery were busy yet fulfilling. She handled everything from setting up displays to guiding visitors through the gallery, explaining the various pieces with an insight that drew people in. Her own artwork hung in a small corner, understated but very meaningful, and she took great pride each time someone stopped and noticed, gazing upon her art. Her paintings, though few, portraits of people she'd met in the city, the places she'd discovered, the emotions she'd felt, were all pieces of her, displayed now for the world to see. Every morning, Rebecca would arrive early to tend to the gallery, carefully dusting frames, adjusting lighting, and setting the ambiance to create an inviting space. She found solace in the quiet rhythm of her tasks, feeling a sense of belonging that had been elusive since she had arrived in New York. This place was her sanctuary of late, her bridge between Southern roots and her dreams in the city. Charlie's presence was more elusive. He would arrive late in the evening after dark, often when the gallery was nearly empty, his footsteps barely audible on the wooden floors. Charlie moved with a quiet grace, his gaze thoughtful, observing every piece of art as if it held secrets that only he could decipher. Rebecca often caught him studying her work, her paintings, his brow furrowing slightly as he examined each brushstroke. When he did speak, his words were measured, almost cryptic, as though he was offering a puzzle for her to solve.

One evening, as Charlie and Rebecca closed the gallery together, he paused by one of her pieces, a portrait of a woman with stormy, turbulent eyes, "You're hiding something in here," he murmured, his fingers grazing the edge of the canvas.

She felt a cool shiver run down her spine, but she forced herself to shrug casually, "Maybe. Aren't all artists always hiding something?"

Charlie's lips curved into a faint smile, "Perhaps, but not all are as adept at disguising it as you are."

Their conversation, though small, brief, lingered in Rebecca's mind long after Charlie had left, planting a seed of curiosity that took root and grew each time they spoke.

As the weeks passed, Rebecca found it harder to ignore the pull she felt toward Charlie. He was nothing like anyone she'd known before, reserved, intense, yet with a kindness that showed in unexpected moments. She couldn't help but feel drawn to his enigmatic nature, the way he seemed to see into the very heart of her art and, somehow, into her soul, as well as her inner desires. One late evening, after closing, Charlie invited her for a drink. "Just a glass of wine, Rebecca, nothing more," he said, his mere tone light but his gaze was penetrating. For a moment, she nearly accepted. She could picture it... the two of them seated in a quiet corner of some dimly lit bar, his voice low as he spoke of art and life, his fingers tracing patterns on the rim of his glass, but she forced herself to shake her head, no. "I'm only here to work, Charlie," she said firmly, ignoring the pang of regret as she turned away.

His expression softened, and for a moment, he looked almost disappointed, but he said nothing, only giving her a slow nod of acceptance. As Charlie left, Rebecca felt a mix of relief and frustration, as if she'd turned away from something beautiful yet seemingly dangerous. Despite the inner turmoil Charlie stirred within her, Rebecca poured herself into her work, her art. Her pieces, her paintings, began attracting much attention, with visitors commenting on the emotion and depth they saw in her paintings. Word of mouth spread, and soon, local art critics were dropping by, making small notes as they moved through the gallery, murmuring amongst themselves. The gallery's modest attendance grew, and Rebecca felt her hidden confidence bloom with each new visitor who lingered by her art corner. But with such success came self-doubt, as she stood before her paintings, she wondered if she was revealing too much of herself, if her vulnerabilities and rawness were becoming too visible. Art had always been her outlet, her escape, but now, it felt more like a confession. The city, with all its relentless pace and harsh demands, had unearthed pieces of her that she hadn't even known existed, and sometimes, the exposure felt overwhelming.

One night, after the gallery closed, Rebecca stayed a little later, lingering by her art corner, lost in deep thought. She didn't hear Charlie enter until he was right beside her, his presence both comforting and disquieting. "They are beautiful, Rebecca," his voice soft, carrying a warmth that sent shivers through her. "But I think there's more, something deeper within you than even this."

She looked up at him, her heart pounding, "I don't know if I can go any deeper, Charlie."

Charlie's gaze was steady, unwavering, "That's where the real art lies, in the depths we are afraid to reach."

The intensity of his words lingered, drawing her in like a strong magnet. Rebecca felt herself inching closer to him, her guard slipping, her carefully built walls beginning to slowly crumble, but just as quickly, she pulled back, a reminder of her main purpose grounding her. "I should go, I think." she murmured, her voice barely a whisper. Rebecca gathered her few things, escaping into the night before she could second-guess herself.

It was only a matter of time before Rebecca's resolve weakened. One late evening, after a particularly long day, Charlie made his invitation once more, "Just dinner. No pressure, no expectations," he said, his mere tone almost pleading, begging, as if he, too, was battling something within himself.

This time, Rebecca couldn't say no, perhaps it was the mere exhaustion, or the thrill of a small victory, but she finally agreed, allowing herself to savor the way his dark eyes lit up when she accepted his invitation to dinner. They met at a small, intimate restaurant tucked away in a quiet corner of the city. The lighting was low, casting a warm, golden glow over the room, and the scent of freshly baked bread filled the air. Charlie ordered a bottle of wine, and they clinked glasses, sharing a quiet toast that held more meaning than either would admit. Their casual conversation drifted from art to life, touching on a hint of childhood memories, dreams, and some vague fears. Charlie's quiet intensity melted, revealing a kinder side, a softness that made her heart ache within her chest. For the first time since she had met him, Rebecca felt like she was really seeing him now, the real Charlie, and not just the enigmatic gallery owner who slipped through the night. At one point, he reached across the small table, his cold fingers brushing hers in a gesture that felt both tender and electric. "You belong here, Rebecca, you know," Charlie murmured, his voice carrying a quiet conviction. "This city... it has a way of pulling the hidden truth out of people, the buried truth, and you have embraced it, more than most."

His words touched her, resonating with a truth she hadn't been able to put into words. Rebecca felt her defenses faltering, crumbling, her mere resolve slipping away under the weight of his intense gaze. For a moment, she allowed herself to imagine what it would be like to just let go, to surrender to the inner feelings she'd been denying. But as the evening drew to a close, she felt a familiar pang of hesitation, a small reminder of why she'd come to New York in the first place. She was here for her art, only her art, her mere dream, and as much as she wanted to explore whatever it was that lingered between Charlie and herself, she wasn't sure if she was quite ready to risk losing it all in someone else. As they walked back to the gallery, the silence between them seemed heavy with unspoken words. When they finally reached the gallery door, Charlie turned to Rebecca, his expression unreadable, "Thank you," he said sweetly, softly, "For tonight."

Rebecca nodded slowly, her heart aching inside her chest, as she turned away, slipping back into the night, leaving him standing at the gallery door, alone.

In the days that followed, something seemed to shift in Rebecca, the conversations with Charlie in the late evenings, the intimacy of the mere night, it had awakened something deep within her, a deeper understanding of herself and her work, her art. She found herself painting with a new intensity, pouring her conflicted emotions into the canvas, capturing both the longing and the restraint that she was feeling. Rebecca's work, her art, grew darker, rawer, each piece a reflection of the complexity of her life in New York. The gallery patrons noticed, their comments tinged with much admiration and curiosity, and her paintings began to draw even more attention. With each brushstroke, she found herself thinking more about Charlie, his words echoing in her mind, urging her to dig a little deeper, to reach for the hidden truth she'd been avoiding. Rebecca couldn't dent the impact Charlie had on her, the way he'd challenge her, pushed her, made her question everything that she thought she knew.

One late evening, as Rebecca closed the gallery alone, she stumbled upon a letter tucked away, behind one of the slightly visible paintings. It was addressed to her in Charlie's familiar, fancy handwriting, a single line scrawled acroos the page, 'Art isn't just about what we create, Rebecca. It's about who we allow ourselves to become, it's about how we truly feel inside."

The words on this small note struck her, resonating with a truth that had been lurking within her all along. In that moment, Rebecca understood what Charlie had been trying to show her, to explain to her, the depth he'd been urging her to explore. She wasn't just here to simply paint her paintings, to create something merely beautiful. She was here to confront her true self, to unravel the parts of herself that she'd kept hidden within, to find her true desires amidst the chaos of the city. As she held the small letter in her fragile hands, Rebecca felt a renewed sense of purpose, a clarity she hadn't known before. She wasn't just an artist chasing a dream, she was a woman discovering who she really is, discovering herself within, piece by piece, brushstroke by brushstroke, and maybe, just maybe, she was finally ready to embrace the light and the shadows that made her who she was.

Night after night, Charlie would return to the gallery, and with each passing evening, their conversations became more intimate, more layered. What started as a shared interest in art transformed into something deeper, conversations laced with philosophy, vulnerability, and curiosity. Charlie spoke with reverence for the old art masters, his words rich with talented knowledge, his voice low and intense as he discussed the emotional depth they captured in their master pieces. He had a way of breathing the life into each story, recounting the tales of such artists who had suffered, who had sacrificed everything for their craft. Rebecca was mesmerized. It was as if Charlie had been there to witness such sacrifices, merely in the way he recited the ancient stories, making Rebecca fell like the art world held many secrets that she'd only begun to glimpse. A small voice in her head kept warning her though, warning her to tread carefully. She couldn't shake the sense that there was more to Charlie than he let her see, layers beneath his reserved demeanor that she could not yet understand, and perhaps, it was that mystery that both drew her in and kept her guarded. There were questions she wanted to ask him, secrets she sensed that he carried like shadows around him, but she held back, afraid that if she pried too deep, he might retreat, might slip away.

One late night, Rebecca stayed behind again after closing, lost in the quiet rhythm of her painting. The gallery was silent, and the only sound was the soft scratching of her brush against the canvas. She sensed his presence before she actually saw Charlie, a faint shift in the air that made her heart quicken. When she looked up, she found him standing a few steps away, his gaze fixed on her with a seductive intensity that sent a massive shiver straight through her. "You're very gifted, Miss Rebecca," he said, his voice low and steady, intimate, laced with much admiration.

Rebecca felt a rush of pride, and her cheeks reddened, flushed with warmth under Charlie's intense gaze, "But you are the one who actually owns this gallery, Charlie," she replied, trying to deflect the compliment with a teasing smile. "You are the one who is actually gifted, talented."

He stepped even closer, his mere expression inscrutable, his eyes dark and unreadable, "I see more than just mere art," he murmured, his voice a soft, intimate caress that wrapped around her like velvet.

His sweet words hung loosely in the air, charged with nervous conviction, and for a moment, Rebecca felt her resolve completely wavering. She wanted to reach out, to close the distance, the gap, between them, but a small part of her held back, uncertain, slightly afraid of what it might mean to truly let him in.

As the weeks passed, Rebecca found herself more and more entangled in Charlie's mysterious world. He seemed to exist on the fringes of normalcy, appearing at odd hours, always shrouded in an air of quiet mystery. There were late evenings when he would slip into the gallery after midnight, just watching her paint in silence before disappearing into the night's shadows, when she would remain after closing for hours working on her paintings. She would glance up, catching only a fleeting glimpse of him, his silhouette framed against the dim glow of the streetlights outside. The more she learned about him, the less Rebecca felt that she truly understood. Charlie would speak of art and history with such an authority that hinted at a life far more complex than he actually revealed.

One night, as Rebecca and Charlie discussed the works of Caravaggio, she asked him where he'd studied art. He hesitated, a faint shadow crossing his face before he replied, "I've had... many teachers."

Something mystic about the way Charlie said it made her pulse quicken, as if he was speaking of another life, a past filled with untold secrets that he could not share. Rebecca wanted to press him for answers to her unspoken questions, to understand the enigma that was actually Charlie, but each time she came close, he would seemingly retreat, his gaze turning distant, his words becoming carefully measured. It was a dance of sorts, a push and pull that seemed to leave her both exhilarated and slightly frustrated. She found herself yearning for his presence, craving the quiet intensity of his hypnotizing gaze, the way he made her feel seen, understood, and yet, there was a part of her that remained wary, a small, faint voice that whispered caution, that seemed to warn her not to let herself fall too deeply into his world, whatever mysterious world that was.

After a particularly intense conversation about Van Gogh, one late evening, and about the beauty found in pain, Charlie invited Rebecca to see a place that he said would 'change the way she saw light'. Intrigued, she agreed, following him through the secluded, dimly lit streets until they reached an old, abandoned, ancient church on the edge of the neighborhood. Inside, the walls were adorned with stunning, larger-than-life frescoes that glowed in the soft candlelight. Rebecca felt a wave of awe wash over her as she took in the mystic details, the colors, the shadows, the way the artist had captured something timeless, eternal. She could feel the depth of all the emotion in every brushstroke that was visible across the vintage walls, the passion and anguish that had gone into each detail.

"This artist understood the light," Charlie said, his voice reverent, "He used it to reveal what lay hidden in the shadows, to show the beauty in the darkness."

Rebecca felt a chill run down her spine as she listened to him, his soothing words touching something deep within her. It was as if he was speaking not only of the art, but of life itself, of the way light and darkness coexisted, each one incomplete without the other. Rebecca turned to look at him, finding Charlie's gaze fixed on her with a quiet intensity that made her heart race. In that moment, she felt an undeniable connection, a sense that Charlie understood her in a way no one else had, and yet, the mystery that surrounded him remained, like a dark shadow that lingered just out of reach. The evening, the night, ended with them sitting on the church steps, the city's lights twinkling in the distance, a soft breeze rustling through the air. Rebecca felt a sense of estranged peace settle over her, a rare calm that she hadn't experienced since arriving in New York. She wanted to hold onto the moment, to savor the quiet intimacy that had grown between her and Charlie. After a long silence, he spoke, almost hesitant, "Rebecca, there are some things about me that... I can't explain. Parts of my life that do not fit into the world you know."

She looked at him, sensing the weight of his words, the struggle hidden behind his calm facade. "You don't have to explain anything to me, Charlie. I just... I just want to know you, understand you."

Rebecca couldn't believe that she had let these words slip from her mouth. Charlie smiled, a faint, bittersweet expression that made her heart skip a beat. "I think you do understand me, more than most." His gaze softened, and for a moment, she felt the imaginary walls between them begin to fall, to crumble into pieces, but just as quickly, the brief moment passed, and Charlie withdrew, retreated, his expression unreadable once more. He stood, his movements graceful, almost ethereal, and extended a hand to her, which was cold as ice, "Come. I will walk you to your home."

As they walked through the darkened streets, their shoulders brushing against each other, Rebecca felt a sense of inner warmth, of belonging. There was something about Charlie that was drawing her closer, but she wasn't quite sure what it was yet. She realized that she was allowing herself to believe that maybe, just maybe, she could let herself trust him fully, that she could step into the darkest of shadows with him and discover the light hidden within him.

Their late-night conversations became a normal routine, the hours spent exploring art and philosophy, began to influence Rebecca's work, her paintings, her art, in ways that she hadn't anticipated. Her paintings grew much more vibrant, richer, each stroke infused with a newfound intensity, a depth that spoke of the emotions she was beginning to explore. She found herself drawn to the darker colors, to contrasts of light and dense shadow that mirrored the complexities she felt inside, that she felt for Charlie. The patrons at Verve Gallery noticed the drastic change, their comments tinged with secretive curiosity and silent admiration. Critics, too, began to take an interest, writing positive reviews that praised her work, her art, for its emotional depth, its raw honesty. Rebecca was no longer the quiet, amateur artist from Alabama. She was becoming someone new, someone who embraced both the light and the darkness that was hidden within her.

Charlie watched as her transformation became one with a quiet pride, his repeating gaze lingering on her paintings each night as they closed up the gallery together. He never commented on the massive change, but Rebecca sensed his approval in the way he would look at her, a silent encouragement that fueled her desire to keep pushing, to keep reaching for something deeper. With each painting, each late-night conversation, Rebecca felt herself falling for Charlie, drawing much closer to him, her emotions entangled with the mystery that engulfed him. She knew she was playing with fire, could feel it, that there were parts of him, his life, that he kept hidden, secrets that he guarded fiercely, but she couldn't bring herself to pull away from him.

As she painted alone in the gallery, late one evening, she felt Charlie's presence once more sneak upon her, a subtle shift in the air that made her heart race. She looked up, meeting his gaze across the room, his face illuminated by the dim glow of the streetlights from outside. There was a tension in his expression, a depth of emotion that she hadn't seen before, a serious countenance across his features. "Rebecca," he said, his voice low and intense, "There's something you need to know."

She felt her heart pound in her chest, a mixture of anticipation and fear twisting in her stomach. She had sensed it for weeks now, a dark secret lurking just beneath the surface, something he'd kept hidden even as they'd grown closer. Charlie stepped closer, toward her, his movements slow, almost hesitant, "I've wanted to tell you... to speak to you for a long time now, but I was frightful, afraid... afraid of what you might think, or what it might mean."

She took a shaky breath, her gaze locked to his, waiting for him to continue.

"The truth is... I am not like other people," he said quietly, his words barely above a whisper, "I've been... alive... for far longer than you can imagine, Rebecca. I've seen centuries pass, watched the world change many times, and yet, in all that time, I have never met anyone like you."

His confession hung in the air, a revelation that seemed to defy everything she knew. She felt a chill run down her spine, her mind struggling to comprehend exactly what Charlie was saying, "You mean... you're..."

He only nodded, an interrupting, faint, almost sad smile on his lips. "I am... I am immortal, a vampire. I have been for a long while, centuries. I've been alone for so long, and I thought that was my only fate, but then I met you, Miss Rebecca, and everything seemed to change."

Rebecca felt her heart race like it was going to burst from her chest, her emotions a whirlwind of shock, disbelief, and for a moment she figured he was teasing her, but his eyes, his dark eyes held some truth to his confession. Then without warning, she felt an overwhelming sense of connection, of an estranged understanding. Somehow, despite the impossibility of his words, she truly believed him. She saw the seriousness in his countenance, in the way his eyes looked at her with a mixture of relief, pain, and of longing with much regret.

"Why... why did you tell me this?" she whispered, nervously, her voice trembling.

"Because you deserve to know the truth of who I really am, you deserve to know the truth of who you are really falling for, Rebecca." he replied, his gaze not faltering, unwavering. "I want you to know the real me, who I truly am."

For a long moment, they stood in silence, their gazes locked together, a world of swirling emotions passing between them. Rebecca felt the weight of his words, the vulnerability he'd revealed, and she knew that this was a turning point, this had been the dark mystery, the secret, he was hiding from her, this was a moment that would define everything that was to come after. Regaining her thoughts, her feelings, she slowly stepped toward Charlie, her heart pounding like a sledgehammer within her chest, as she closed the distance between them. Slightly fearful, yet calm, she reached out, her warm, fragile hand trembling, and touched his ice-cold face, her fingers grazing his cool skin. In that moment, she felt the emotional connection between them, the depth of his inner battles, the loneliness he had carried for many years.

"I'm not sure what this means," she whispered, her voice barely audible, with small teardrops swelling in her eyes, "But I really want to find out. I want you, only the man that I have learned to respect and possibly love."

With those words, Rebecca felt a sense of peace within, as it settled over her, a quiet certainty that, despite the darkness, despite the mystery, she was exactly where she was meant to be. She saw in Charlie's eyes, a small blood tear forming and she knew exactly, that he felt the same way.

Months drifted by, and Rebecca found herself helplessly in love with her immortal man, drawn to Charlie's enigmatic allure, now that he could truly be himself in front of her. She had resisted for so long, even told herself that she was only here to focus on her art and nothing more, but each passing night seemed to pull her heart closer to him. Charlie was magnetic, an unspoken challenge that tugged at her very soul, an invitation to explore a part of herself she hadn't known existed. After several hours spent talking beneath the soft glow of the art gallery lights, Rebecca agreed to go anywhere with Charlie, if he wanted her to. Deciding to try another date, instead, they strolled through the quiet streets of the city, laughter mingling with the cool night air. With him, she felt like the city was theirs alone, like she was safe from any type of harm, a vast, mysterious canvas waiting to be painted, explored, yet even in these lighthearted, romantic moments, Rebecca sensed something much darker beneath the fine surface, an intensity in Charlie's gaze that remained, reminding her of the secrets he'd possibly been keeping from her.

Spending more nights together, drifting from shadowed cafes to secluded corners of the park, Charlie would vaguely tell her stories of the city's past, of his past, of artists who had dreamed, haunted these streets long before she was born. He painted pictures of the lives lived in much passion, of tragedies and triumphs woven into the very fabric of New York. Yet, he would never answer her one question... 'How was he made into an immortal, a vampire?'

Rebecca felt herself falling, slipping deeper into his world, her romantic attraction growing with each story that Charlie told, each lingering glance he would give her, but there was an estranged darkness that clung to him, an almost predatory tension that she couldn't quite ignore. As much as she tried to brush it aside, a part of her remained wary, as if he were a beautiful flame and she was a helpless moth.

One night, they found themselves in a quiet cafe, sharing a bottle of deep red wine. The dim light cast shadows across Charlie's pale face, accentuating the sharp lines of his masculine features, his dark, hollow eyes catching the glow with an intensity that made her shiver within. She could no longer hold back the question that haunted her since his revelation, "What are you hiding from me, Charlie?" she asked gently, her voice stern, yet sweet.

He did not respond at first, his distant gaze drifting to the wine glass in his hand. Finally, he met her eyes, a faint smile playing at the corners of his mouth, "Sometimes, shadows are more revealing than the light," he replied cryptically, the hint of a hushed challenge in his tone.

Rebecca, determined, held his gaze, sensing the weight of his words, the unspoken truth lurking just beneath the surface. She knew he was a vampire, he had already told her that much, but she also knew that he hadn't told her everything. He'd left out pieces of the puzzle, pieces of his life, parts of himself that he kept hidden, as if afraid of what she might see if she looked too closely.

"I trusted you, trusted you with even my life," she said, her voice firm but laced with a hint of vulnerability, "But you haven't told me everything, have you?"

Charlie hesitated, a flicker of something, of pain, regret, crossing his face. "I didn't want to frighten you, to scare you, Rebecca. There are... needs that come with this immortal life, things that I've learned to control, but control does not erase them."

The realization hit her, sharp and undeniable. She thought back to the stories she'd heard, the myths and legends of vampires, of the thirst for human blood that defined their mere imaginary existence. Charlie had told her about his vague life, about the centuries he'd witnessed, but he hadn't mentioned the blood hunger he struggles with, the primal urge that he had tried to keep hidden from her. Rebecca's pulse quickened, a mixture of fright, fear, and something different, a strange, twisted fascination that she could not shake. She knew exactly what Charlie was, knew he was a vampire, but it just didn't seem realistic until now, and yet, their strong connection between them lingered like a haunting melody that she could never escape.

That night, Rebecca left him alone, in the restaurant, without a word, the weight, the reality, of his blood lust confession pressing down on her, suffocating her thoughts. She returned to her apartment, her mind a chaotic swirl of emotions, fear, betrayal, longing. She had known, in some distant part of her mind, that this was the truth, Charlie did survive on blood alone, human blood. She'd sensed the mere darkness in him, felt the edge of his restraint, but actually hearing it aloud made it far too real, brought her face to face with such a reality that she wasn't sure how to accept.

Days passed, and she threw herself into her art, her paintings, pouring her confusion, her anger, her frustration, her longing onto the canvas. Her work became much darker, more visceral, the colors more raw and violent. She painted late into the night, her hands aching, her heart heavy, saddened, each stroke a desperate attempt to exorcise the emotions that threatened to consume her.

Charlie didn't come to the art gallery during those days, and though Rebecca told herself she was grateful for the needed space, she couldn't help but feel his absence like a hollow ache in her chest. She missed his quiet presence, his insight, the way he seemed to understand her without any words. She missed him, but she also knew that if she saw him again, she would be forced to confront the truth of what he really was, a killer, a vampire, and she wasn't quite sure if she was ready to face it just yet.

One late evening, after nearly a week without a word from him, Rebecca returned to the art gallery after closing, feeling a strange sense of restlessness. She wandered through the darkened rooms of the gallery, her faint footsteps echoing against the wooden floors, the quiet solitude pressing down on her. She was becoming miserable without Charlie in her life. Then, she felt it, that familiar shift in the air, a subtle presence that sent a chill down her spine. She turned to find him standing at the entrance, his pale face cast in shadow, his mere expression unreadable. "Rebecca," he murmured, his voice low, laced with such emotion.

She took a shaky breath, her heart racing in her chest as she met his gaze in the faint darkness of the place, "Why are you here, Charlie?"

Stepping closer, his movements slow, cautious, as if he was afraid of startling her, "I happen to own the place, Rebecca, and because I could not stay away. I wanted to give you time, space... but I cannot pretend that I don't feel this... this love I have for you, I cannot act like I don't want this."

Rebecca held his gaze, the vulnerability in his dark, hollow eyes disarming her, weakening her resolve. She felt the weight of her emotions pressing down on her, the tension that had simmered between them for so long, it seemed, finally reaching a breaking point.

"It feels like you lied to me," she said, her voice barely audible, barely above a whisper, "You kept those things from me. The truth about how you survive."

Charlie's expression softened, slight regret flickering his gaze, "I did not want to burden you with my true past, with the darkness that comes with it, but you were so persistent on wanting to know the truth, and I cannot lie to you. Please, know that I would never hurt, or harm you, in anyway, Rebecca. I've spent many, many years learning to control my hunger, trying to deny it. I never wanted to be... a monster, but I was made against my own will."

His words hung in the air, a sincere confession that cut through her anger, her frustration, even her fear. Rebecca saw the pain in his hollow eyes, the years of struggle and restraint, the weight of an immortal life lived in the shadows, and in that moment, she realized that he was as much a prisoner of his nature as he was a master of it. He had chosen to resist, to deny his blood hunger that merely defined what he was. She seen that he did not enjoy succumbing to it. Slowly, Rebecca took a step forward, her hand reaching out, brushing against his, "Charlie, I do not know if I can fully understand... but I am willing to try."

His gaze weakened, fragile with a flicker of hope lighting his undead eyes, "I never wanted you to bear this burden, Rebecca. I never wanted you to see, to know that side of me. I only wanted you to see, to know, me... the man I once was inside, not the fiend I am now. But if you are willing, I will be here, I will be whatever you need me to be."

With those last words lingering in her mind, the distance between them dissolved, replaced by an estranged connection that ran deeper than either of them could have imagined, love.

From that night on, Rebecca and Charlie's relationship took on a new intensity, a depth born from the shared understanding of Charlie's true nature. Rebecca never asked about his blood lust again, she'd rather leave it hidden. They spent countless hours together now, talking, exploring new parts of each other. Rebecca learned more of his past, his childhood, about his family that he once had. She discovered things he shared with her about the past centuries he had witnessed, about the people he had met and loved, yet lost. She could almost visualize the scars left by a life lived in such isolation, the loneliness that haunted him despite his quiet strength. In turn, Charlie listened to all her stories, her fears, her doubts, the insecurities that she had carried with her since she was a child. She told him about her childhood, her family, and being raised in Alabama. He would laugh and say, "Well, that explains the accent..."

Charlie would encourage her to face her fears, her doubts, to always confront the parts of herself she had been so afraid to acknowledge, and in doing so, Rebecca felt a new sense of inner freedom, a liberation that allowed her to express herself more fully, both in her art, her paintings, and in her life. Her paintings transformed, becoming richer, brighter, more vibrant, each piece a mere reflection of the small journey she'd taken thus far, the connection she'd forged with a man, a vampire, who existed on the fringes of frail humanity. The patrons of the art gallery, Verve Gallery, noticed the drastic change, and soon her art, her paintings, began to attract attention from more critics, collectors, even other gallery owners from other parts of the city. Some of the gallery owners who had rejected her were demanding to have her art displayed in their galleries now. Despite the sudden success, the growing recognition, Rebecca found herself longing for the quiet moments spent with Charlie, the conversations that revealed new layers of their mere souls. She realized that her art, her true passion, had grown from the connection she shared with him, from the trust they had built in the face of their differences.

One late evening just after nightfall, Rebecca and Charlie walked through the city after visiting an art exhibit, where her few paintings were being held on display. Charlie stopped, turning to her with a look of quiet intensity. "There's something I need to show you," he said, his voice tinged with a strange weakness.

He led her to a secluded part of the city, a small rooftop overlooking the skyline, the lights of New York stretching out before them like a sea of stars. As they stood together, the wind howling, rustling through their hair, Charlie reached into his coat, pulling out a small, worn notebook. "These are my sketches," he said softly, embarrassed, handing them to her. "My way of... preserving the people, the moments of my past, that have touched me. My way of remembering, even when time has taken everything else."

Rebecca opened the fragile, worn notebook, her breath catching as she flipped through the faded pages. The faint sketches were beautiful, haunting, each one capturing a face, an unforgotten memory, a moment that has been frozen in time. She saw the traces of his past life in each line, the emotions that he had carried with him through the many centuries, and then, on the last, final page, she saw a drawing of herself, her face captured in delicate detail, her expression one of a quiet strength, vulnerability, hope. Rebecca looked up, meeting his stare, her heart pounding with love, "Charlie... I don't know what to say."

Charlie reached out, his cold hands brushing against hers, his dark eyes filled with such emotion that took her breath away, "You've changed me in ways you will never know, Rebecca. In ways I never thought possible. You have given me a reason to hope, a reason to enjoy life again, to believe that there can be something... more, even for a creature such as I."

Rebecca felt a surge of unspoken emotion, a sense of clarity that washed away her doubts, her inner fears. As small drops of tears swelled in the corners of her eyes, she knew that their love, their connection was truly real. That it was worth fighting for, despite the shadows that vaguely lingered between their worlds. In that moment, she made a choice, a silent vow to embrace both the light and the darkness within Charlie, to always stand by his side, no matter what the future held. As they stood together on this rooftop, beneath the endless expanse of the night sky, Rebecca realized that she had found something, found love, that she hadn't known she was searching for.

A love that transcended time, a bond forged in the shadows, the darkness, a mere connection that would guide her through the unknown.

In the days that followed, Rebecca felt a new sense of purpose, a determination to embrace the life she had chosen, to explore the mere depths of her art and her heart. She knew that the journey ahead would be filled with new challenges, that there would be moments of unsettled doubt, fears, but with Charlie by her side every night, she felt a peacefulness, a resilience that carried her forward. Together, they would step into the unknown, a path filled with both light and shadow, a journey that would sometimes test them, challenge them, and ultimately reveal the true nature of their souls. For Rebecca, it was the beginning of a new chapter in her life, a story that would be written in vibrant colors, in brushstrokes, in the language of love and art and eternity.

As the months flew by, Charlie began to fear the mere thought of losing Rebecca. He pondered on how he would live for eternity, and how she would one day, pass away, out of his immortal life, leaving him alone. In a desperate act of protection, he offered Rebecca a choice. As many dangers loomed in various ways that she could not understand, Charlie felt that he could no longer bear the thought of her being so vulnerable, mortal, at risk in this world that he inhabited. His voice was calm but weighed with much emotion with centuries of past regrets as he spoke, "Rebecca, there are things I cannot protect you from. This life... it comes with its own risks, its own demands, but if you choose, you could join me in this immortal life, live beside me forever, never parting."

Rebecca's heart pounded in her chest, the reality of his words sinking in. She had never let it cross her mind that she would someday leave this world and Charlie would be alone. She understood that to be with him fully, truly, she would have to step completely into his world, surrendering her mortality, her mere humanity. Her mind whirled, slight fear clashing with an aching desire to never leave his side. She had never been afraid of the mysteries he embodied, but the overall thought of leaving him behind, alone, and the mere thought of leaving her human life that she had only known, friends, family, the warmth of the sun, the passage of time to grow old, was nearly paralyzing.

"Think carefully, Rebecca," he urged gently, "Immortality is not a freedom. It's a prison. I want you to understand the truth of such a gift, a curse. An eternity in darkness comes at a great cost." Charlie's hollow eyes betrayed a different truth, a longing that matched her own, a flicker of hope, yet great fear, a longing that perhaps, together, they could bear it.

She searched his intense gaze, seeing the nervousness beneath his ageless exterior. In that moment, Rebecca's longing overpowered her thoughts. The choice was no longer one of logic but of the heart. "I choose you, Charlie," she said, her voice steady yet trembling, "No matter what the cost might be, I choose to be with you, forever."

And so, within the quiet shadows of the Verve Gallery, surrounded by the many paintings that had once represented her dreams, Rebecca let herself be transformed, allowing herself to be an immortal, a monster, fiend, a creature of the night. She felt her soul and body yield to something both terrifying and exhilarating, as if every sense were heightened, every emotion sharpened. The thrill of immortality rushed through her, intoxicating and all-consuming, as Charlie graciously bit her neck sinking his fangs into her vein. Afterwards, he offered her his immortal blood, as she greedily sucked it from his wrist. Her old life slipped away, only a memory now, and with it, the boundaries of mortality she had once known.

As the days turned only to nights, Rebecca embraced her new undead existence with Charlie guiding the way. Their love, fueled by this newfound bond, grew more intense as they explored the city in twilight, weaving through its secret places, finding beauty in the world that only those who walked in darkness could see. The thrill of such immortality, the freedom to wander the city's depths without any fear of time, without any fear of aging, was exhilarating. They became like mere phantoms, ghosts of the city's forgotten hours. They shared their art together, they painted together, using abandoned buildings as their canvases, leaving behind images of passion, despair, and longing. They dined on rich wines and fed on the blood of unwilling strangers, indulging in their shared desires, their mere needs. Charlie taught her how to take only what she needed without truly harming every victim, how to drink the blood from a human in a way that left only a faint memory, like a touch of ecstasy, lingering in their mortal minds. Their love grew stronger, deeper, a shared exploration of the dark shadows within each other now. They would stand on rooftops as dawn approached, watching the city transform, its hidden world replaced by daylight's harsh, unforgiving glare. Quickly, they would slip into darkened rooms before the sun's rays actually touched the earth, safe in each other's arms, sharing a love as ancient as the night itself.

But even as Rebecca savored her new life with Charlie, she began to notice a strange darkness creeping back into Charlie's hollow eyes. He would disappear from her for hours without explanation, returning with a haunted look in his eyes, a shadow of despair that he couldn't fully hide from her. She would ask him what troubled him, and he would shake his head, offering only a faint, sorrowful smile. "It's nothing," he would only say, brushing her fragile, pale cheek with his cold fingers, "Just the weight of an old life trying to creep back in."

This weight Charlie secretly carried was more than just memories, it was a deep darkness born of centuries ago, an accumulation of much pain, betrayal, and many regrets. Rebecca could see it in his distant gaze, in the way he would stare at the paintings they had created together. His hollow, dark eyes clouded with something she could not reach. She felt a growing sense of helplessness, unable to pull him from the depths of his past sorrows that he kept hidden within.

One late night, after a long silence, Charlie finally spoke to her of his past, what was haunting him so badly. They sat together in the art gallery, surrounded by Rebecca's paintings that she was working on, each one bearing a slight trace of his mere influence, his guidance. "Rebecca, you know of the things I have seen, what I have told you, shared with you, the life I have lived in the past, but I haven't told you about the things I've done," he began, his voice barely a whisper, "The innocent people I have hurt along my eternal journey, the lives I've taken... those memories never really fade, they haunt you always. These memories haunt me, like ghosts that I can never escape. The innocent children that I massacred, the innocent women I misled to their ruin, their death."

Rebecca listened, shocked at his sincere confession, her heart breaking for him as he recounted all the early years of his immortality, the utter darkness that had consumed him as he struggled to understand his new nature that was placed forcibly upon him. There had been no one to guide him, no one to show him how to balance the blood hunger with humanity. He had lived as a mere predator, surrendering to his blood lust desires, until the weight of his own sins nearly drove him mad. Sometimes these inner demons arise within him, almost overpowering him. "I have tried so many times to redeem myself, to live without such guilt," he murmured, "But the past... it still clings to me, like a shadow I can never fully shake."

Rebecca reached out, her hand resting on his pale face, but he pulled away from her touch, his gaze distant, "You deserve better, Rebecca. Someone who can love you without this conviction, this guilt, this mere darkness inside them. I know you are much stringer willed than I am, but you need to be truly loved by someone who can have less guilt when they look into your beautiful eyes."

"I chose you, Charlie," she said, sternly with confidence, her voice filled with conviction, "I chose you, knowing all of this, whether it was brutal or good, and I still choose you."

Even as she spoke, Rebecca saw the despair in his hollow eyes, the way he seemed to be slipping further from her grasp, lost, consumed, by a past she could never reach.

In the nights that followed, Charlie's inner darkness, his inner torments, grew even more consuming. He withdrew from her, spending long hours just wandering the city alone. His once-steady presence now replaced by a fragile, haunted version of himself. Rebecca tried to reach him, to pull him back from the edges, but each attempt only seemed to push him further away. She watched helplessly as Charlie descended into utter despair that consumed his very existence, his laughter fading, his smile faltering, his hollow eyes losing the spark that had once made her feel so alive. She tried to remind him of their everlasting love, of the immortal life they had built together, but he was slipping too far, like sand falling between one's fingers.

One cool night, Charlie came to her, after a long silence, his heavy eyes dark and empty with his expression hollow, "I just can't do this anymore, Rebecca," he said, sadly, "I thought I could, thought I could suppress these demons inside me. I thought that our love would be enough to pull me from these darkened shadows, but I am... I am lost. They have overtaken my undead spirit now."

Rebecca felt her heart shatter, a deep ache radiating through her as she took in his broken expression, "Charlie, please... we can get through this, together. Just let me help you!"

But he shook his head, his gaze filled with a haunting sorrow that cut her to the core, "I was a fool to believe that I could actually escape my haunting past, that I could overcome this hurtful guilt, that I could be anything other than the true monster I am."

And with that, before Rebecca could respond, he was gone, disappearing into the night, leaving her alone in the art gallery that had once been their exciting sanctuary.

Many nights passed without any word from Charlie, and Rebecca felt the hollow ache of his absence, a disturbing void that consumed her with each passing night. She searched the city, hoping to find him, to bring him back, but he was nowhere to be found. Each empty night felt like a lifetime, a cruel eternity without him by her side. 'Where are you, Charlie?' She would roll over and over in her mind.

Then, one late evening, she returned to empty gallery to find a single letter resting on the paint table next to her latest work of art. Charlie's handwriting scrawled across a fancy envelope with her name written on it. Her hands trembled as she opened it, her heart pounding as she read his words...

Rebecca,

I wanted to give you the immortal life that you truly deserved, a life filled with much love, beauty of the night, and light under the moon, but I see now that I am only utter darkness, evil. Only a mere shadow that will always consume those who come to close. You are much stronger than I ever was, and you have the power to live this undead life in a way that I never could. Although, you are immortal, you still have a 'love' for all humanity, never lose that. The art gallery is yours, along with everything within it. Build it into something miraculous, something beautiful, something lasting. Keep my sketchbook close to your undying heart. Forgive me for leaving in this way, for failing you, my love. Know that you were always the only light in my darkness, my eternal night. You were the only 'love' I had ever truly known in my immortal existence. I must go now; I have a date with the sun...

Charlie

The letter slipped from her cold fingers, and she sank to her knees, a raw, aching, painful sob escaping her lips as blood tears rolled down her pale cheeks. The weight, the reality, of his loss crashed over her, a grief so profound that it felt as if her heart were being torn apart. She felt the emptiness of eternity settle over her, the harsh realization that she was now truly alone in the world of the night. Charlie was gone, forever.

In the weeks that followed, Rebecca carried on, she took over Verve Gallery, honoring Charlie's memory by filling it with the art they had painted, had created together, and with art that spoke of their love, their loss, their brief but intense journey together. She painted him as she remembered him, haunted, beautiful, a man consumed by hidden shadows but filled with a depth that she had truly loved with every part of her undead soul. Her portraits of him that she had painted, drew crowds, people drawn to the sadness, the raw emotion, the sorrow that bled from every stroke. Critics hailed her work, her masterpieces of Charlie, as a new era in art, a depth of feeling that captured the essence of the human experience, of love and great loss, and the fragile nature of time. But for Rebecca, it was not merely art. It was a way to keep Charlie with her, to hold onto his memory, the memory of the man, the vampire, she had loved, even as she walked alone through this darkness of eternity.

As the months flew by, Rebecca learned to navigate her secret, immortal life alone. She became a fixture in the city's art scene, a mysterious figure who only appeared at nightfall, her gallery, which was once Charlie's, was now a haven for those who sought art, beauty in the darkness. She became known as the 'Lady of Verve', a woman whose haunting beauty and sorrowful gaze captivated everyone who crossed her path. Even as she embraced her successful role, even as she grew into her mere immortality, she never forgot Charlie. He remained within her, tucked deep inside her undead heart.

On the quiet nights, Rebecca would stand on the gallery's rooftop, gazing out at the city that her and Charlie had once explored together, remembering all the laughter, the whispered promises, the moments of such connection that had defined her life. She had become a creature of the night, an immortal bound to the darkness, but she still carried Charlie's memory like a light within her, a reminder of the love that had forever changed her entire existence. Within her heart, he was not just a mere memory, not just a shadow of the past. He was the one who had given her eternity, success, the one who had help to express her inner talents, he showed her the beauty and the pain of a life lived within such darkness, and as she continued this immortal journey, painting the story of their love on the walls of the Verve Gallery, she knew that he would always be a part of her, a presence that always lingered like the stars, a dim light in her eternal night.

Several years passed, and Rebecca transformed Verve Gallery into a sanctuary for those searching for meaning in the chaos of art and existence. Each exhibit told a story, echoing the layers of her own tale, a dance between light and shadow, love and loss. She vowed to never reject anyone who had the hunger for art, for dreaming of something better in their lives, just as she did once.

When the nights seemed to grow long, in the quiet moments, she would feel Charlie's presence linger, as if he were a ghost haunting the gallery. Though the art gallery thrived, the emptiness of his absence always loomed large, a void that no canvas could ever really fill. One late night after the gallery was closed, Rebecca was hanging a brand-new collection from an amateur artist, when she stumbled upon an old sketch of Charlie's, one she hadn't seen in years. His raw talent, beautiful and dark, struck her like a wave. In that moment, the weight of her actions pressed down, as a blood tear swelled in the corner of her hollow, saddened eyes. She felt the nedd to honor him, to share more of his story, not just as the man she had lost but as the artist he truly was. With each brushstroke across the canvas, she poured out her undead heart. The piece depicted their first night together in intimacy. The backdrop of the painting was the gallery alive with color, their laughter intertwining with the music of the city. She painted him as he was, flawed, tragic, and fiercely alive. It was a love letter to the darkness they had once shared.

The next night, the exhibit opening drew a massive crowd, with many local reporters snapping pictures with their flashy cameras, everyone was buzzing with anticipation as the doors opened to the gallery. As people and critics admired her art, her work, along with several new, amateur artists, Rebecca knew that Charlie would never truly leave her. She knew he would be very proud of what the art gallery stood for now, and the success it was bringing to others. His legacy, his spirit would live on through her art, forever intertwined in the shadows and colors of her immortal life.

At last, the night drew to a close as the last guests departed, Rebecca stood alone in front of the entrance, the art gallery bathed in moonlight. She closed her hollow eyes, feeling the cool air swirl around her. In the silence of the night, she looked up at the vague sky and whispered, "Charlie, I miss you, I thank you." The words hung in the air, a secret promise that the love they shared would echo on through time, even in the depths of the darkest of nights. And with that, Rebecca embraced her own darkness, ready to paint her future into the unknown, an eternal canvas, forever shaped by the tragic beauty of love lost. Charlie would always be remembered... their love story, their tragic tale, will always linger on through all eternity...

    The End

Poem: Love of Art & Loss

Love of Art & Loss
I loved you once like brush to paint,
With strokes so deep they carved my fate,
But colors fade, and hands grow faint,
Now art is all I consecrate.

You haunt me still in charcoal hues,
In whispered lines, in shaded views,
Where I, the artist, paid my dues,
To every piece I couldn't lose.

Each portrait holds the ghosts I know,
The light I chased, now lost below,
A flickered smile, a fading glow,
In shadowed frames where memories grow.

FOR THE LOVE OF ART

The love I knew now sits in oils,
In turpentine and soiled spoils,
A beauty scarred by all my toils,
A palette made of ashen soils.

So here I paint with haunted grace,
To trace the lines of your lost face,
While darkened pigments find their place,
In love's abandoned, empty space.

And though my art still breathes of you,
It fills no void, it heals no bruise,
Just endless colors I must use,
To paint a love, I'll always lose.

For The Love of Art

By: Anna Elizabeth